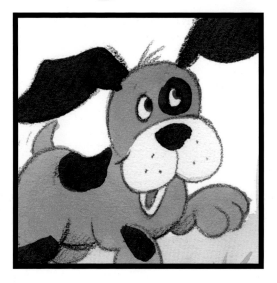

written by
Kathleen Urmston

illustrated by
Gloria Gedeon

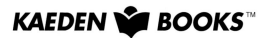

Sammy likes to play.

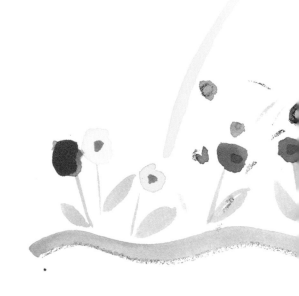

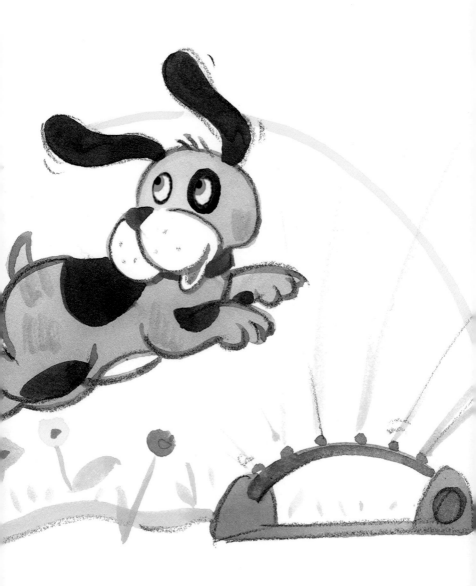

Sammy likes to run.

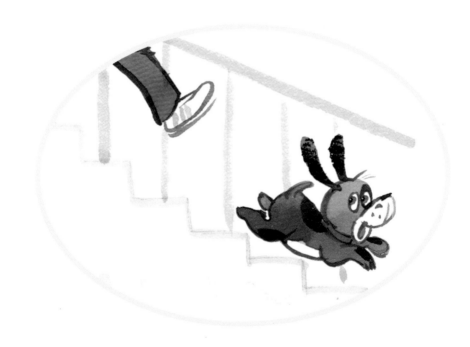

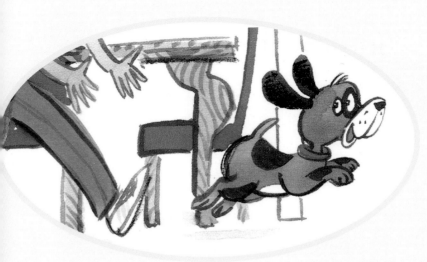

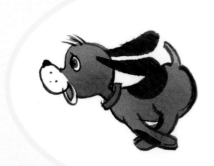

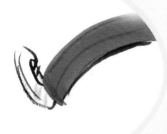

Sammy likes to hide.

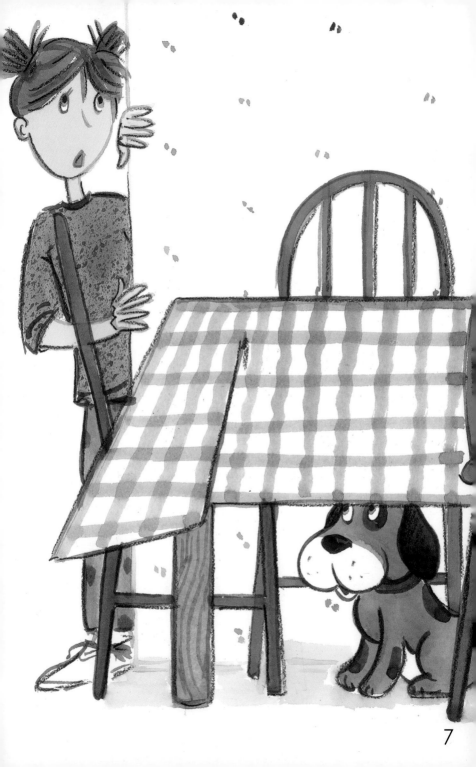

Sammy likes to bark.

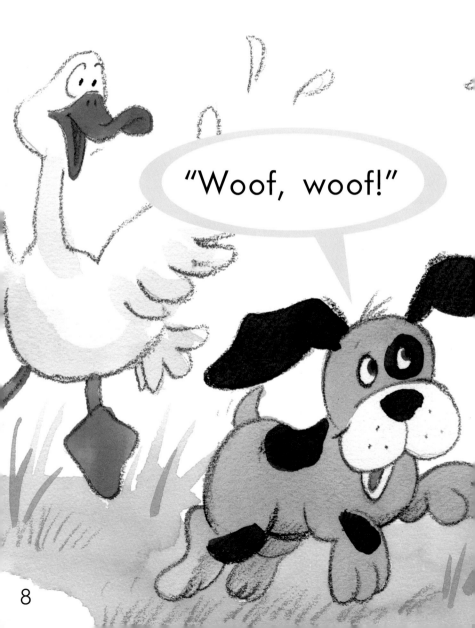

"Woof, woof!"

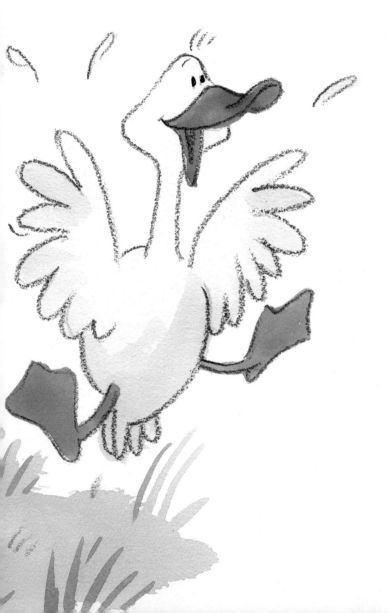

Sammy likes to ride.

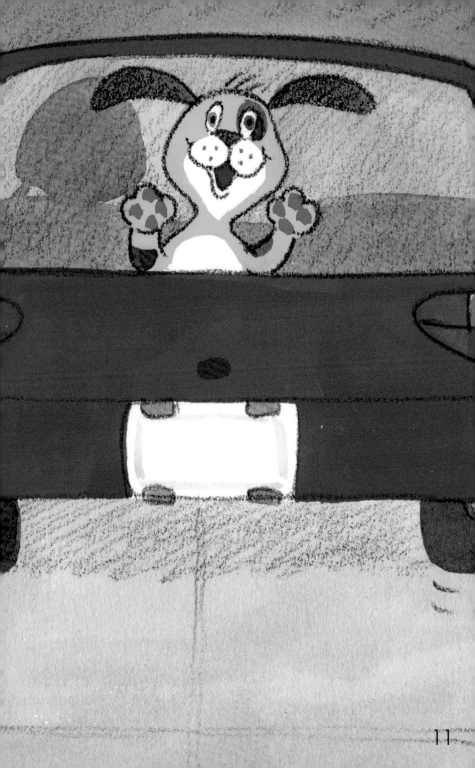

Sammy likes to jump.

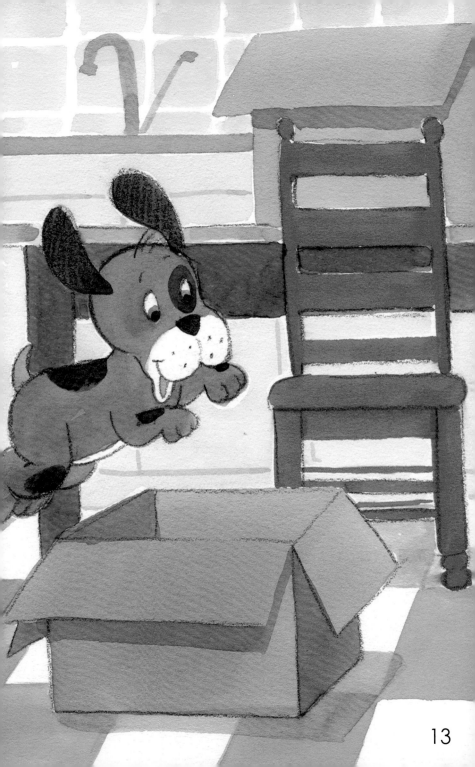

Sammy likes to dig.

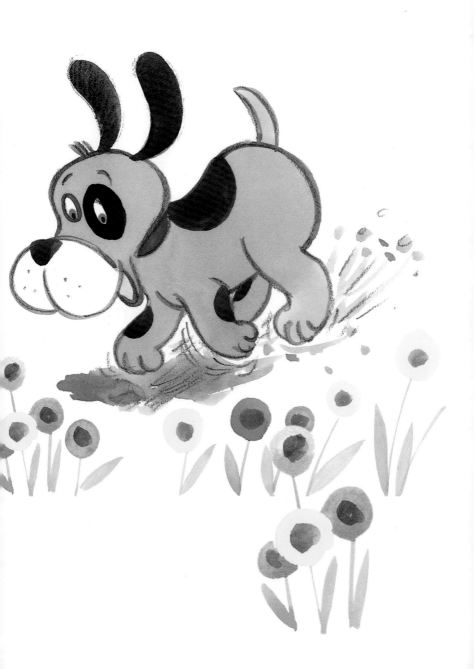

Sammy likes to sleep.

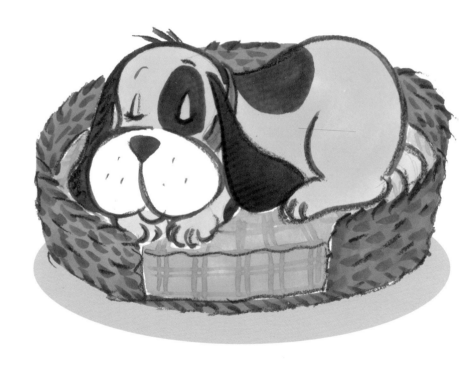